The Fairy House
Fairy Riding School

Welcome to the Fairy House –
a whole new magical world…

Have you got all *The Fairy House* books?

- ☐ FAIRY FRIENDS
- ☐ FAIRY FOR A DAY
- ☐ FAIRIES TO THE RESCUE
- ☐ FAIRY RIDING SCHOOL
- ☐ FAIRY SLEEPOVER
- ☐ FAIRY JEWELS
- ☐ FAIRY PARTY
- ☐ FAIRY FLYING LESSONS

Make sure you visit www.thefairyhouse.co.uk
for competitions, prizes and lots more fairy fun!

The Fairy House
Fairy Riding School

Kelly McKain

Illustrated by Nicola Slater

■ SCHOLASTIC

For Evie, with love

First published in the UK in 2007 by Scholastic Children's Books
An imprint of Scholastic Ltd
Euston House, 24 Eversholt Street
London, NW1 1DB, UK
Registered office: Westfield Road, Southam, Warwickshire, CV47 0RA
SCHOLASTIC and associated logos are trademarks and or registered trademarks of Scholastic Inc.
This edition published in 2009

Text copyright © Kelly McKain, 2007
Illustration copyright © Nicola Slater, 2007

The right of Kelly McKain and Nicola Slater to be identified as the author
and illustrator of this work has been asserted by them.

Cover illustration © Nicola Slater, 2009

ISBN 978 1 407 10889 6

Printed in the UK by CPI Bookmarque, Croydon, CR0 4TD
Papers used by Scholastic Children's Books are made
from wood grown in sustainable forests.

1 3 5 7 9 10 8 6 4 2

This is a work of fiction. Names, characters, places, incidents and dialogues are products
of the author's imagination or are used fictitiously. Any resemblance to actual people,
living or dead, events or locales is entirely coincidental.

www.kellymckain.co.uk
www.scholastic.co.uk/zone

Chapter 1

Katie hurried out into the garden as soon as she got home from school. She ducked under the wire fence and on to the patch of rough ground beyond. The afternoon sun shone down and the almost-meadow was alive with insects buzzing round the wild flowers and butterflies fluttering in the breeze, but Katie hardly noticed. She swished through the tall grass determinedly, heading straight for

the old oak tree. She had to see her new friends, and quickly. She needed to ask their advice. She had a feeling she'd just done something very silly indeed.

As she reached the oak tree, with the dolls' house beneath it (now beautifully decorated and renamed the Fairy House) she saw her friends, busy enjoying the lovely sunshine.

When Katie had left her pink plastic dolls' house out under the old oak tree by accident, she'd never imagined that four fairies would move in!

They'd had such wonderful times together – dancing and singing and playing fairies' games and making things and having adventures. She'd even become a fairy herself and had a go at flying, and she'd rescued Daisy from the clutches of the revolting Tiffany, a horrid girl in her class. It was, in fact, precisely this horrid girl that Katie now needed to speak to the fairies about.

Shy little Snowdrop was watering her window boxes, her black hair tumbling forwards over her pale face as she leaned out of the window. Daisy was sunbathing in a

3

handkerchief hammock they'd rigged up between two sticks, a dreamy smile on her kind face. Flame-haired Rosehip and cheeky Bluebell were happily practising acrobatics in the shorter grass under the tree, with their cute fairy skirts tucked into their underwear (and for once they weren't arguing!).

Katie giggled as Bluebell's shock of blue hair stood on end when she did a handstand.

"Hi, Katie, come and play!" she called, from upside down.

Katie smiled but shook her head. "Maybe later," she said. "Right now I need your help – all of you!"

She stepped carefully over Daisy's hammock and put her little finger on the doorknob of the Fairy House, which Bluebell had bewitched with fairy dust. "I believe in fairies, I believe in fairies, I believe in fairies," she whispered.

The top of her head tingled and there was a familiar whooshing sound in her ears as she shrank down to fairy size. Then she sat on the bench of woven grass and

twigs that Bluebell had made and her fairy friends gathered around her.

"What's wrong?" asked Daisy.

"Well, you know Tiffany made me write her story for her?" she began and the fairies all nodded, crossly. Katie knew they were still angry about Tiffany bullying Katie into doing her homework, and worse, about pinching the Fairy House – with poor Daisy still in it!

"Well, you know that Tiffany's father had promised her a pony if she got a star for the story?"

They all nodded and Rosehip muttered, "Not fair!"

Katie folded her arms tight. "Well, she did get a star, and a pony! Now she's challenged me to take part in a gymkhana this Saturday at her stables."

"What's a gymkhana?" asked Snowdrop.

"I think it's a competition where you play lots of mounted games," said Rosehip, her eyes gleaming. "We had one at the summer festival in Fairyland, and I got to ride one of the Fairy Queen's ponies, remember?"

"Oh, yes!" cried Bluebell. "Do you think it will be the same sort of thing for humans, then?"

"Probably," said Rosehip. "And it's great fun. You lucky thing, Katie!"

But Katie didn't feel like a lucky thing. "That's the problem," she mumbled. "I've never ridden a pony in my life. I don't even know how!"

"Oh, right. So obviously you said no to Tiffany," said Rosehip

blithely. "I mean, mounted games are fun but if you don't know how to ride you'd almost definitely fall off and hurt yourself and—"

Listening to this, Katie went pale. "Actually, I said yes," she told her startled friends.

"But why on earth would you do that?" Daisy asked, all concern. "As Rosehip said, it could be dangerous."

Katie took a deep breath. "While Tiffany was talking I noticed that she had a new ring on," she told them. "It had a pale green stone in it, and I'm sure it's peridot! That's one of the birthstones we need to complete the fairy task."

The fairies' eyes all grew wide then. The fairy task was the reason that they were here. They needed to complete it before they were

allowed back into Fairyland.

"I made her promise that if I competed against her and won, she'd give me the ring," said Katie. "If I get it we'll be one step closer to saving the tree."

Daisy gasped and Bluebell said, "Good thinking, Katie – and wow, you're so brave."

Snowdrop drew the scroll she'd been given by the Fairy Queen from her pocket and unrolled it. Once again, they all peered over her shoulder to read it. They did this every day, just to remind themselves of the importance of what they had to do. Secretly, they all hoped that some magical new instructions might appear there to make the task easier, but nothing ever did. The scroll read:

Fairy Task No. 45826

By Royal Command of the Fairy Queen

Terrible news has reached Fairyland. As
you know, the Magic Oak is the gateway
between Fairyland and the human world. The
sparkling whirlwind can only drop fairies off
here. Humans plan to knock down our special
tree and build a house on the land. If this
happens, fairies will no longer be able to
come and help people and the environment.
You must stop them from doing this terrible
thing and make sure that the tree is
protected for the future. Only then will you
be allowed back into Fairyland.

By order of Her Eternal Majesty
The Fairy Queen

PS You will need one each of the twelve
birthstones to work the magic that will save
the tree - but hurry, there's not much time!

A few days had gone by since they'd last got a birthstone and the fairies were all starting to worry. Katie lay awake at night sometimes too, frightened that the bulldozer was revving up that very moment, ready to come and knock down the tree. They knew that Tiffany's father, a builder, was behind the wicked plan. But until they had all the birthstones they were powerless to stop him. Without all twelve, they wouldn't be able to work the magic to save the oak tree, and Fairyland with it.

So the fairies could easily understand why Katie had decided to challenge Tiffany in order to try winning one of the birthstones. But that didn't make it any less dangerous.

"But surely your mum won't let

you?" mused Snowdrop.

"She's said I can go, even though neither of us like Tiffany, because she knows how much I love ponies. But she does think I'm only having a beginner's lesson," she admitted, blushing.

"Which race do you have to beat Tiffany in?" asked Rosehip nervously.

"The Chase Me Charlie," said Katie.

"Oh, I haven't heard of that," Rosehip said.

"I'm sure it's easy-peasy," said Bluebell helpfully, but Katie didn't feel any better.

"Maybe you could look in it up a book?" Daisy suggested.

"Good idea," said Katie, "I'll have a look in the school library tomorrow. It's a pity I can't learn how to ride from a book, too! What

on earth am I going to do?"

"Maybe we can help," said Rosehip suddenly. "You remember when you took the Fairy House inside and we got a little bit, well. . ."

"Naughty, and so we wrecked everything," finished Bluebell.

"Well, we brought your toy ponies to life with fairy dust, didn't we?" Rosehip continued, thoughtfully. "I was just thinking that if we brought them out here and, well, there's not much time, but maybe—"

Katie leapt to her feet, suddenly under-standing her. "We could bewitch them to come to life and you could teach me to ride!" she cried.

"Wow, Rosehip, that's brilliant!" gasped Snowdrop.

"Well, don't get too excited, there's hardly any time and –" Rosehip was saying. But Katie didn't hear her, she'd already grabbed the enchanted door handle and was busy turning big. "Back in a moment!" she called, as she rushed off to get the ponies.

For the first time since she'd agreed to the gymkhana, Katie felt a rush of excitement about it. Rosehip's riding lessons would give her a chance against Tiffany. Only a teeny tiny chance, of course, but a chance all the same.

Katie knew she had to try.

After all, they really needed that birthstone.

Chapter 2

A few minutes later, Katie was back at the Fairy House with the toy ponies, a bottle of water that Mum had insisted she bring out, and a blue cotton bag bulging with something mysterious. She had also changed out of her school uniform and into jeans and a T-shirt.

"Good thinking," said Rosehip, nodding towards her clothes. "Much better for riding."

"What's in the bag?" asked

Bluebell, who couldn't bear not knowing *everything, straight away.*

Katie smiled, knelt down carefully and tipped the contents of the bag out on to the grass. The fairies gasped at the array of pony care equipment in front of them. There were grooming brushes and combs and ribbons and elastics. It all looked great, except. . .

"Oh, no, there's only one bridle and saddle set," Snowdrop wailed.

The fairies' wings all drooped with disappointment.

"We were hoping to all learn together," said Daisy sadly.

But Bluebell didn't give up that easily. After a moment she picked up the bridle and studied it, then said, "Don't worry, I can make these from daisies and we can ride bareback!"

"You clever thing, Bluebell!" Snowdrop cried, and they all cheered up again.

Katie stood the five plastic ponies (well four ponies and one unicorn!) up on a flat piece of grass. Once she'd taken hold of the enchanted doorknob and turned small again, it was time to get down to work.

While Daisy helped Bluebell to gather daisies for the bridles, Rosehip and Snowdrop made an

arena of twigs and woven grass around the ponies to ride in.

"If we're bewitching them with fairy dust to come alive, they're going to need water, just like real ponies," said Rosehip. "I wonder how. . ."

But Katie soon had a good idea about that. She and Snowdrop went into the Fairy House and up to the bathroom. Together they dragged the bath down the stairs (fairies don't have baths and they'd thought the tub was for mixing potions or playing hide and seek in!). They set it up just beside the arena and, with Daisy's help, they carefully tipped up Katie's water bottle and filled the bath right to the top, making the perfect pony drinking trough.

Then Daisy had the idea of making safety hats from the early

unripe conkers on the horse chestnut tree near the edge of the almost-meadow. Bluebell flew up to get them, then stamped on the green shells to open them up (she was very good at stamping!).

Soon everything was ready, and it was time to enchant the ponies – Katie and the fairies were so excited they couldn't help dancing round on the spot and squealing with joy! Snowdrop took the tiny bottle of fairy dust from her pocket and walked nervously up to the white unicorn, who she'd ridden when the fairies were naughty in Katie's house. She stroked his mane and gave him a longing look.

"That one can be yours," Katie told her, smiling. "He's called Moondust."

Snowdrop beamed at Katie, then

shook a little of the fairy dust into her palm and rubbed it on to the end of the unicorn's nose. From mane to tail, he rippled with a sheen of sparkles, and then suddenly he was a real live unicorn. He whinnied with glee and nuzzled up to Snowdrop, looking very pleased to see her again.

For herself, Katie chose a pretty pink pony called Rainbow, with a multicoloured mane and tail. She could hardly believe that only

yesterday she'd been playing with him in her bedroom – she'd never have imagined that she would get to ride him! When she rubbed the fairy dust on to his nose he came shimmering to life, then whinnied and trotted happily around the arena.

Next, Bluebell chose the blue pony with the purple mane and tail, who Katie said was called Damson. Daisy took the yellow one, Sunshine, with her pure white mane and tail, and Rosehip got Poppy, a beautiful orange pony who licked her hand almost as soon as she rubbed the fairy dust on to her nose.

Then Katie heaved the saddle off the arena fence and strode purposefully towards Rainbow. "We have to get started straight away," she told Rosehip anxiously. "Mum

will be calling me in for tea soon and there's so much to learn."

But Rosehip just smiled at her. "You need to get to know your pony first and make friends," she said. "So put that saddle back and grab a grooming brush."

Katie felt very lucky that she had a friend who could really show her the ropes, and soon they were all busy grooming their ponies. Daisy made Sunshine's tail into two plaits with daisy bobbles just like hers, and Snowdrop combed out Moondust the unicorn's mane until it was sleek and shiny. Bluebell flicked Damson's purple mane and tail out to match her own hair and Rosehip styled Poppy's into cascading waves. As for Katie, she weaved some pink ribbons into Rainbow's tail and then tied her own hair up with the rest.

Then Rosehip said it was time to ride, and Katie felt a flutter of nerves and excitement in her chest as she hurried back to the fence to get the saddle and bridle.

Rosehip helped them all to put their bridles on, and showed Katie how to do up the buckles under the saddle. Then, with the conker-case helmets safely strapped on, they mounted up, ready to start their very first riding lesson.

They began by walking round the edge of the arena, with Rosehip leading the way on Poppy, calling out instructions. After a while, Katie was getting the hang of turning Rainbow at the corners so that they

didn't keep ending up stuck at the fence. Everyone was getting on very well, except Bluebell. She loved the riding, but she didn't like being told what to do by Rosehip. Not one little bit.

"Why can't *I* be the teacher?" she whined.

Rosehip wheeled Poppy round and trotted expertly up to Bluebell. "Because it was my idea and also because I'm the only one who has ever ridden before!" she said.

"Still doesn't mean you know *everything*!" Bluebell grumbled.

"Bluebell, just stop complaining, sit up straight and shorten your reins," ordered Rosehip, which seemed to annoy Bluebell even more!

Katie was far too excited to grumble about anything. She was

getting to ride a pony for the very first time, and it felt amazing. She'd always wanted to have a go, but they'd never quite had the money for lessons.

Katie beamed – riding was just so much fun, especially when Rosehip showed them how to do trotting. Katie seemed to bump around a lot more than the fairies, who naturally moved with the ponies' rhythms, so Rosehip showed her how to use her stirrups to stand up and down. It took a while to get it right, but once she did, she just couldn't stop grinning – she was starting to feel like a real rider.

Poor Snowdrop wasn't having such as easy time, though. Moondust was keen to go galloping off and she had to keep pulling the reins to slow him down. And Daisy was having

the opposite problem, as Sunshine would hardly go anywhere! Instead she kept dropping back to walk and wandering over to the edge of the arena to munch at the grass.

"Come on, Daisy, you're supposed to be in charge of that pony!" shouted Rosehip, but Daisy didn't seem too worried – she was just as dreamy as Sunshine!

Katie was having so much fun that she almost missed Mum calling her in for tea. Reluctantly, she leapt off Rainbow and gave him a big pat for being so good. Then she raced back over to the Fairy House, grabbed the enchanted doorknob and tingled and whooshed herself big again. She called goodbye to her friends as she hurried away, promising them that she'd come back straight after school the next

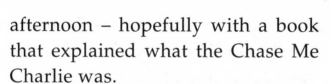

afternoon – hopefully with a book that explained what the Chase Me Charlie was.

Katie came back through the kitchen door with a heart full of joy and a head full of ponies, ponies, ponies! Thanks to her wonderful friends, she might *not* actually fall off in the competition!

And maybe, just maybe, she might have a teeny-weeny chance of beating Tiffany.

Chapter 3

The next afternoon, Katie arrived at the Fairy House with a library book clutched in her hand. She put the book down on the grass and then turned small as her friends hurried out to greet her.

"I found this book! It says in the index that the Chase Me Charlie is explained on page thirty-five," she told them with a grin.

Together they flicked through the pages, which were as tall as them.

"This is great!" Rosehip exclaimed. "It explains all the gymkhana games, and they *are* a bit different from fairy ones. Can you leave it with us, Katie, so I can read up on what to teach you?"

"Of course," said Katie. She thought again how lucky she was to have Rosehip for an instructor.

When they reached page thirty-five, they all knelt over the book in trepidation.

"In the Chase Me Charlie the competitors jump over higher and higher poles," Rosehip read aloud. "If you knock a pole down you're out. The last person left in is the winner."

Katie stared at her, shocked. "But Rosehip," she cried. "I hardly know how to ride *at all*, let alone *jump*! What on earth am I going to do?"

She looked so panicked that Bluebell and Snowdrop quickly pushed the book shut, to stop her staring at the photograph of a girl and pony leaping over an enormous red and white striped pole. Daisy put her arm round her trembling shoulders and said gently, "Don't worry, you don't have to do it. It sounds far too dangerous. Just tell Tiffany that you're not competing and we'll find another way of getting the birthstone."

Katie really wanted to back out, but she shook her head. She couldn't let the fairies down. "Thanks, but I promised I'd help you in any way I could, and that's what I'm going to do," she told them. "This could be our only chance of getting that stone. I've got to go for it."

"Good for you, Katie," cried Bluebell. "You know you can do it!"

"And look how quickly you learnt to trot. I'm sure you'll be jumping in no time!" said Rosehip encouragingly.

Then the fairies all hugged Katie, and said how brave she was. She wasn't so sure about that, but she had to learn to ride, and she was determined to do her best. She forced the dreaded Chase Me Charlie to the back of her mind, and concentrated on trotting Rainbow

around the arena behind Snowdrop and Moondust.

"Why can't we canter yet?" Bluebell called out to Rosehip, swinging her legs back and forth impatiently.

"Let's just spend a bit more time trotting first," Rosehip said firmly.

But Bluebell didn't want to spend a bit more time trotting first – Bluebell wanted to canter! And nothing Rosehip said was going to stop her.

She gave Damson a hefty kick in the sides and the pony flew forwards into canter, past the others, heading straight for the fence. Bluebell shrieked in fright and shouted, "Abandon pony!", leaping off just as he jumped. She shot into the air, turning somersaults, flapping her wings desperately, but

she just couldn't get control. She tumbled downwards and landed with a splash in the water trough!

The fairies and Katie gasped, but when Bluebell emerged, blowing out a big mouthful of water like a fish in a  fountain, they all burst into peals of laughter.

After some more trotting Rosehip said, "Bluebell has kindly demonstrated the *wrong* way to go into canter. Now I will show you the *right* way," and she and Poppy romped round the arena in perfect rhythm.

When Katie tried, she thought it was the most amazing feeling she'd ever had in her life – easily as good as becoming a fairy and flying.

After several more canters, it was time to head home. Katie had had so much fun she couldn't help grinning to herself all through dinner. When Mum asked what she'd been doing, she replied, "Oh, nothing much, just playing with my toy ponies in the almost-meadow. I made an arena and pretended to have a riding lesson and learnt how to canter and everything!"

Mum beamed. "That's great, darling. And when you go to the stables on Saturday you'll get to ride a pony for real!"

"I bet it will be brilliant fun," said Katie, still smiling to herself. She couldn't tell Mum that she'd just

been riding a pony. Like most adults, Mum couldn't see fairies – and so she was unlikely to believe that Katie was being taught to ride an enchanted pony by one.

She just hoped that Rosehip really could get her jumping by Saturday.

When Katie came swishing through the tall grass of the almost-meadow the following afternoon her friends were already busy in the paddock, and they waved and called out greetings as she approached. Her stomach flipped with excitement as she paused by the Fairy House to turn small and then hurried over to them.

"Oh wow!" she cried, dashing up to Daisy, who was busy painting a stick with blue and red stripes. "They look just like the jumping poles in my book!"

"Yes, we've been busy all day building things for the gymkhana games!" said Bluebell proudly.

Katie saw that they'd brought the plastic chairs out of the kitchen, and Rosehip and Snowdrop were busy painting them with matching stripes.

Just then, Rainbow trotted up and Katie made a big fuss of him, patting him and ruffling his mane. The other ponies were happily milling around the paddock, chomping on grass and drinking from the water trough that Bluebell had fallen in.

Grinning, Katie grabbed a brush and started helping Daisy paint the jumping poles.

Soon everything was ready, so Katie and the fairies gave their ponies a good brush and put their bridles on. Then it was time to ride!

As they mounted, Katie felt her nerves and excitement thrumming in her chest.

"Let's start with the Chase Me Charlie," said Rosehip, as they walked their ponies round the arena, warming up. "After all, that's the game you need to beat Tiffany at to get the birthstone, so that's the one which matters most."

Katie gulped – the Chase Me Charlie was also the scariest game

by far, as she'd have to do jumping. But she was determined to try her best – she really didn't want to let her friends down.

Rosehip sprang expertly off Poppy and set up the jump. She balanced a stripy pole on the lowest rung of two chair backs and put another on the ground below, as a guide for the ponies.

Then they all lined up to have a go at jumping it.

Rosehip went first, to show them how it was done. She and Poppy leapt effortlessly over the pole and landed at a canter on the other side. Bluebell volunteered to go next. She raced up to the pole and made a good jump, except for the big wobble on landing! But the pole stayed on, which meant she was still in the game.

Then Snowdrop and Moondust had a go – and Moondust leapt so high over the pole that Snowdrop had to cling on for dear life!

"I forgot to mention that unicorns are excellent jumpers!" called Rosehip, as Snowdrop caught her breath.

"If only I could ride *Moondust* in the gymkhana, I'd easily beat Tiffany!" said Katie with a sigh, making them all giggle.

"Can you imagine her face if you came riding out on a unicorn?" chuckled Bluebell.

It was fun to imagine – but of course, they all knew the birthstone had to be won fair and square. Turning Moondust big and riding him in the gymkhana was hardly that!

Next, Daisy and Sunshine trotted

lazily over the pole and it thunked to the floor.

"You're out because you knocked the pole down," Rosehip told Daisy, but Daisy just smiled and let Sunshine's reins slide through her hands so that the pony could eat the grass. Neither of them seemed to care about jumping higher anyway!

Katie took a deep breath. There was no more putting it off. Everyone else had jumped and it was definitely her turn. She gathered all her courage and they cantered towards the jump. But at the last minute she lost her nerve and pulled on her rein so that Rainbow swerved away.

Rosehip was really kind and said she could have a second try, but Katie just made Rainbow swerve out again. Her hands were shaking

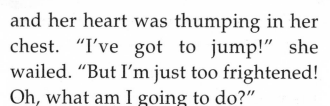

and her heart was thumping in her chest. "I've got to jump!" she wailed. "But I'm just too frightened! Oh, what am I going to do?"

"Why don't we try some of the other games," Rosehip suggested. "Getting upset about the jumping will just make it harder."

Katie agreed, feeling relieved.

The gymkhana games turned out to be really good fun. They played musical chairs, with Rosehip singing fairy songs as they rode in a circle around the painted kitchen chairs. When she stopped they all had to leap off their ponies and dash to sit down. They were having so much fun that Bluebell didn't even complain when she was first out, and happily helped Rosehip with the singing instead.

Then they set three chairs out in

two lines and took turns to weave round them to the far end of the arena and back again, just as it showed in the book. Katie and Bluebell were neck and neck as the first pair, but with Moondust galloping at top speed, Snowdrop pipped Daisy at the post.

Then they did the flag race and Daisy said she'd be the judge so Rosehip could have a ride. Katie raced Snowdrop to the end of the paddock  to grab a coloured flag each and when they got back they tagged Rosehip and Bluebell, who both set off at a furious canter! They played this game over and over just for the fun of it, and soon Katie was really enjoying zooming across the arena and whizzing round in a tight turn at the end.

When they finally paused for breath, Katie remembered the more serious matter in hand – beating Tiffany. But there was no time to try the Chase Me Charlie again – she'd promised Mum she'd be in after an hour, because they were off to visit Auntie Jane.

There was no avoiding the jump on Friday afternoon though – the gymkhana was the very next day, and it was Katie's last chance to try the Chase Me Charlie. As soon as she got to the almost-meadow and turned small, she hurried straight to the paddock. Her friends were already mounted and trotting round on their ponies, warming up. She

called to them, "This is my last chance to practise, so I guess I'd better have another go at that Chase Me Charlie." Then she strode over to Rainbow to get him saddled up.

So Katie tried the Chase Me Charlie again and again, but she was still too scared to jump, and every time she failed, she just got more and more upset with herself. Then when she finally *did* force herself to go over, with her eyes tight shut and squealing in fright, Rainbow got confused and knocked the pole with his back hoof. Rosehip said well done for going over at all. She wanted Katie to have another try but suddenly Mum was calling her in for tea and their time was up.

Katie dismounted and gave Rainbow a big pat. After all, he'd

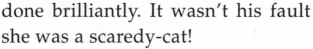

done brilliantly. It wasn't his fault she was a scaredy-cat!

"Can't you just magic it so that I win?" Katie asked her friends desperately, trying one more time to find a way out of doing the gymkhana.

The fairies shook their heads. "That's too big a spell for us," said Daisy sadly.

Katie glanced hopefully at Rosehip. "Or, I know, you could turn big and do it *for* me, like when Bluebell took my place at school," she suggested.

But the little fairy just gave her a hug and said, "Sorry, Katie, but Tiffany challenged *you*, so you have to do it yourself. Otherwise even if we win, you won't be entitled to the peridot ring."

Katie sighed. There was no way

round it. She *had* to ride against Tiffany. She hugged her friends goodbye, turned big again, and with a heavy heart trudged back towards the garden fence.

After tea she told Mum she was extra tired and went upstairs early, still feeling upset. As she lay in bed, she wondered how on earth she was going to even get over the first jump in the Chase Me Charlie, let alone actually win it!

Chapter 4

The next morning, Tiffany's nanny Lisa picked Katie up and she sat alone in the back seat of the car – Tiffany had insisted on sitting in the front, of course, which suited Katie fine.

As she gazed out of the open window her stomach churned with nerves and excitement about the gymkhana. Then suddenly she gasped – the four fairies were zooming alongside the car, waving

at her! She put her hand out of the window and they clung on as she pulled them in. They fell into her lap in a panting, tousled heap – not used to flying so fast!

"Surprise!" cried Bluebell. "We're coming to watch!"

Katie beamed in delight – with her friends there to support her, things would be much more fun.

"And you'll need some proper riding clothes for the gymkhana," Rosehip said. "You can't go in those scruffy jeans and old school shoes."

The fairies exchanged cheeky looks and, with a sprinkling of fairy dust, Katie's clothes shimmered into fabulous smart riding gear, all pink and purple. She had a real safety helmet and shiny black riding boots and everything. As Katie gazed down at herself in disbelief,

Daisy whispered, "Katie-ella, you shall go to the gymkhana!"

They all giggled at that and as Katie joined in, Tiffany turned round sharply in her seat, forcing the fairies to duck down out of sight. Her eyes widened when she saw Katie in her smart new clothes. "How did you do that?" she demanded. "What happened to your scruffy jeans?"

Katie shrugged. "I quickly got changed. I had my riding things in my bag. Erm, it's amazing what you can find in the village jumble sale if you look hard enough," she added

quickly, in case Tiffany began asking where she got them.

"You might look the part but you'll never beat me in the Chase Me Charlie," said Tiffany petulantly, then turned back round, sulking.

The words "Chase Me Charlie" sent Katie into a panic. "I can't go," she hissed, as the fairies flew up from the footwell. "I can't do it."

"You'll be OK," said Daisy gently. "Just do your best."

"But do make sure you win, won't you?!" added Bluebell cheerfully. "After all, the future of your world *and* Fairyland depends on it!"

"Bluebell, be quiet!" cried Snowdrop, but Katie knew she was right. They needed to collect all twelve birthstones to save the tree and here was a chance to get one.

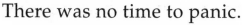

There was no time to panic.

They turned into the stables and the car stopped. Tiffany got out and marched away up the track, not even waiting for Katie. Heart pounding, Katie got out too and thanked Lisa for the lift. Then she tramped towards the office, with the fairies flying high above her so they wouldn't be spotted. She was about to walk in when she noticed Tiffany standing by the desk, so she hid round the corner and peeked inside. The fairies fluttered silently through the door though, and landed on a beam high above Tiffany's head.

"*There*," Katie heard Tiffany say to herself as she wrote something on a list. "Let's see how little miss perfect Katie gets on with Ebony. If she *can* get on, that is! He's so fierce

she'll probably be thrown off before she's even in the arena. There's no way she's having my peridot ring!"

And with a nasty laugh she marched out of the door.

Katie pressed herself behind it, breathing hard. What a sneak! Tiffany had put her down for an impossible pony! She should have guessed she'd do something like this, just to make absolutely sure Katie wouldn't win.

Katie felt utterly terrified and the confidence she'd built up with her fairy friends in the almost-meadow ebbed away. As they flew out of the office to meet her, she looked into their faces, hoping to see encouraging smiles, but they looked just as worried as she did, even Rosehip.

Katie gulped. She knew that was a bad sign.

A very bad sign indeed.

The fairies and Katie had spent the last few minutes peeking over the stable door at Ebony – and trembling.

Finally Katie found the courage to open the door, but she'd only taken one step inside when the pony began snorting and pawing the ground, teeth gnashing. Terrified,

she squealed and shot back out again, smack-bang into a very smug-looking Tiffany. "Enjoying your pony, are you?" she asked, pretend-innocently.

"How could you do this to me?" Katie cried. "There's no way I can ride *him*!"

Tiffany just smirked and said, "Looks like you'll have to pull out of the gymkhana, doesn't it?"

Just then, Katie caught a glimpse of her friends doing something that appeared to involve fairy dust and silent chanting above Tiffany's head. As soon as Tiffany had stalked off, she demanded to know what they'd been up to.

"Oh nothing!" Bluebell giggled. "We've just put a fairy spell on her, that's all."

Katie narrowed her eyes at them,

worried. "What fairy spell?" she asked, but the fairies just grinned, looking very cheeky indeed.

"Oh nothing important!" said Daisy breezily. "Just a little something to make sure that if you do win, she plays fair and gives you the ring."

"Now, let's get on with grooming your pony," said Rosehip. "We don't have much time."

Katie stared at her. "Are you crazy?" she cried. "There's no way I'm going in that stable!"

Rosehip nodded. "I understand. Don't worry, I'll go in first and have a little word with Ebony."

Katie was completely confused by this. "A little word?" she repeated. "How can you have a little word with a *pony*?"

Rosehip just grinned at her and

flew into the stable – only the slight tremble in her wings gave away the fact that she was nervous too. The other fairies perched on the stable door to watch and Katie peered in, from a safe distance.

Rosehip fluttered slowly up to Ebony and landed on the water bucket. Katie started to worry that he might simply knock her in and drink her up, but instead he just lowered his great black head and snorted at her.

"Rosehip, take care!" Katie whispered in alarm as she watched her friend climb up the pony's velvety mane and lie flat along it, so that her head was up by his ear.

Then she began to whisper to him

so quietly that Katie couldn't even catch the words, pausing every so often to listen to his snorts.

"Ebony's saying that the owner of the stables is trying to sell him because he keeps bucking and rearing and dumping riders on the ground," Rosehip said softly.

Katie stiffened, frightened. She didn't like the sound of that one little bit!

"But no one will buy him because he's so bad tempered," Rosehip continued, stroking the pony's ear.

As Rosehip whispered and listened, Ebony's snorts became gentler and gentler until they were just soft whinnies. His whole body seemed to relax and Katie felt that although no fairy dust was involved, she was watching a very special kind of magic indeed.

"He's saying that he's only naughty because he's lonely and bored," Rosehip told them.

"Poor Ebony!" sighed Snowdrop.

"Never mind poor Ebony!" Katie cried in panic. "What about poor *me*? He just told you he likes to dump riders on the ground!"

But Rosehip just giggled. "Don't worry," she said, "he's promised to be good for you this afternoon."

Katie's heart gave a little leap of sympathy for Ebony after that. Nervous of him as she was, she certainly knew what it was like to feel lonely and bored. Before she'd met her fairy friends, she'd had to fill long hours playing by herself.

"And he says that all he wants is to get out of this yard where nobody likes him, and find one special little girl to love," Rosehip added.

"Ahh!" said the other fairies.

In no time, Ebony was far more relaxed. Rosehip gave his ears a final stroke and then flew back to the stable door as he began contentedly munching on his hay.

Katie stared in at Ebony. She still didn't completely trust him, but she had to try. Scarcely daring to breathe, she opened the stable door and stepped inside. But this time Ebony just nuzzled her hand in greeting, and allowed her to lead him out of the stable and tie him up in the yard.

Soon she was happily grooming him until his black coat shone, and

putting ribbons in his mane and tail, just as she'd practised on Rainbow. When she'd finished he looked like the handsomest pony in the world. Rosehip gave her a hand to tack up and suddenly she found herself swinging up into Ebony's saddle and heading towards the main yard.

As she rode to her place at the far side of the arena, Katie tried to swallow her nerves and be a good sport, saying, "Good luck," to the other riders as she passed them. They all smiled and wished her luck too, except Tiffany, of course. At first she looked shocked to see Katie riding at all, then she sneered, "You may have managed to get on that pony, but you'll never *stay* on!"

But Katie didn't reply. The whistle

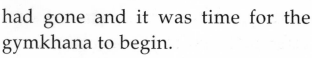

had gone and it was time for the gymkhana to begin.

And Tiffany was wrong – Katie did stay on!

They played similar games to the ones that she'd practised with the fairies in the almost-meadow, and Ebony was a dream, doing exactly as she asked him to and really trying his best. She soon forgot any worries and started enjoying herself, especially when she caught sight of the fairies, sitting on the arena fence nearest to her, and cheering her on, each hidden behind a piece of bunting!

Katie was really cheered up by the look of surprise on Tiffany's face as she and Ebony picked up a third place in the bending race (round cones not chairs this time, but the idea was the same). And Tiffany's surprise soon

turned to annoyance when Katie and Ebony also came joint-second in the flag race with a girl called Irum.

When the first round of games was over everyone dismounted and had a drink of water. Tiffany said to Katie, "I don't know how you've made that pony behave but believe me, it won't last. He'll be back to his old tricks in the Chase Me Charlie, and then you'll be on the ground! Just you wait!"

Katie tried to ignore Tiffany's unkind words, but she couldn't help feeling upset. Her stomach twisted with nerves as she watched the jump being set up. But even if Ebony did behave (and she really hoped Rosehip was right and Tiffany was wrong about that!) she had no idea if she'd clear the first jump . . . or be brave enough to try at all.

Chapter 5

Katie took a deep breath and tried to stop her hands from trembling on the reins. It was time for the Chase Me Charlie. There were three other girls up against her in their age group – Tiffany, of course, and Sophie and Bhavan, who'd introduced themselves as they all waited for the jumps to be set up. They both said they'd done lots of jumping before, which made Katie even more nervous.

Then the judge signalled that the competition had begun and they all lined up for the first round.

The first pole was very low and the others all effortlessly jumped clear. Then it was Katie's turn. She closed her eyes and squealed as Ebony trotted over the pole, hardly seeming to notice that it was there. It wasn't a great performance, but the pole stayed up and she was still in the game.

As she trotted Ebony past the fairies on the fence, they all gave her a big clap and she managed a wobbly smile. Her heart was thumping hard – she'd got over the first jump. Now she just had to keep going.

In the next round, Sophie misjudged the distance and knocked the pole down, which shocked

everyone. But Katie managed to get over again, and this time it was with her eyes open, so she was able to steer a bit better!

Then, with the three of them left in, the pole was moved up again.

As she waited her turn, Katie reached down to give Ebony a big pat

and he snorted happily – he was being absolutely brilliant. There were no traces of his past character left at all, and he seemed to be enjoying the competition enormously.

However, one person who wasn't pleased with his performance was Tiffany, and as Katie neared the third pole, she shouted, "Stop, there's a bee on you!" really loudly.

For a fleeting moment, Katie panicked, but then she realized that there was no bee and that Tiffany was just trying to put her off. That only made her more determined to succeed and she jumped clear again!

But so had Bhavan and Tiffany, and the pole went up again. Katie ruffled her pony's mane and said to him, "Come on, Ebony, let's show them what we're made of!"

This time, she cantered at the jump and cleared it easily. Her stomach flipped with excitement and she couldn't help smiling. They were doing it – they were actually doing it! The only problem was that Tiffany and Bhavan cleared it too, so they had to keep going.

In the next round, the pole went up again and this time the height made Katie gulp, especially when Bhavan knocked it down and went out.

Only she and Tiffany remained, going head to head for first place.

Tiffany gave Katie a nasty look, then booted her pony into canter and went awkwardly over the jump – for a moment the pole wobbled and Katie thought it was going to come off. But no such luck! She had to go again. This was really

getting high and she wasn't sure whether they'd make it.

As Katie cantered round the corner and lined herself up with the pole, she was so busy thinking about the height of it that she looked at the ground as they went over instead of forward and had a big wobble. With a huge effort of will and a steadying hand on Ebony's mane, she managed to get her balance back – the pole stayed on and so did she – but only just! She felt despair creeping in – she and Ebony only made it over by the skin of their teeth. They'd

definitely be out on the next round.

Bluebell whistled and Katie looked towards the fence as she rode back to the start line. The fairies had all picked dandelions, which they were now using as pompoms, singing, "Katie, Katie, Ra-ra-ra, Katie is a superstar!"

That certainly made her smile! She felt her confidence coming back, knowing how much her friends believed in her.

As Tiffany turned towards the fence she said to Katie, "I'm going to win, so you may as well give up now. I'll just keep jumping higher and higher until you and that useless nag lose!"

Katie instinctively leaned over to hug Ebony's neck – he wasn't a useless nag, he was a fabulous star pony! When Katie looked up again, Tiffany was heading for the jump. But she made a clumsy approach and as they took off, her pony's back foot knocked the pole. It wibbled and wobbled and then – thunk! – it was on the ground.

Katie stared at it. She couldn't believe it. Tiffany was out! All she had to do was jump this final pole to win!

As she gathered her reins, Katie caught sight of the fairies peeking

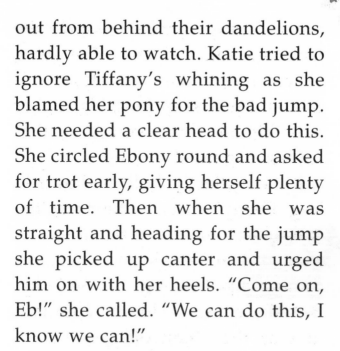

out from behind their dandelions, hardly able to watch. Katie tried to ignore Tiffany's whining as she blamed her pony for the bad jump. She needed a clear head to do this. She circled Ebony round and asked for trot early, giving herself plenty of time. Then when she was straight and heading for the jump she picked up canter and urged him on with her heels. "Come on, Eb!" she called. "We can do this, I know we can!"

They neared the jump and she gritted her teeth and bobbed forward. Ebony flew over and . . . they'd won!

Katie gave a shout of joy, and Ebony whinnied and cantered her past the fairies so quickly that she couldn't even turn her head to see them. She heard their cheers,

though, and Bluebell singing the ra-ra-ra song.

Everyone in the small crowd was clapping as Katie slowed Ebony to a trot, then a walk. She caught sight of a girl about the same age as her, with short dark hair, clapping especially hard. Ebony was watching her too, and Katie wondered who she was.

Then she noticed the organizer coming towards her, so she dismounted, shook hands with him and received her red rosette, which she tied proudly on to Ebony's bridle. When Tiffany was handed the second place rosette she didn't even say thank you. The organizer was still standing there beside them and

Katie realized they were supposed to shake hands. She offered hers to Tiffany, who reluctantly took it.

"Well done," mumbled Tiffany, looking away.

"Thanks," said Katie brightly. "You too."

"I can't believe you did that!" Tiffany added. "I thought you'd never ridden before."

Katie just grinned. "Beginner's luck, I guess," she said, with a twinkle in her eye.

Then she turned and led Ebony out of the arena and back to his stable, almost skipping with sheer delight, the fairies flying high above her. Once they were safely out of sight, the fairies zoomed down and swamped Katie in hugs and congratulations.

"Thank you all for helping me,"

said Katie. "Especially you, Rosehip."

"It was nothing," said Rosehip, but she was glowing with pride.

After they'd all made a huge fuss of Ebony too, Katie went to claim her winnings.

She found Tiffany by her pony's horsebox, sulkily grooming him while telling him off for not winning.

"I've come for the ring," Katie said.

"What?" Tiffany replied, without looking up. "I don't know what you're talking about."

Katie felt queasy. She'd won fair and square – surely Tiffany would have to give it to her. "You promised," she said weakly.

"Sorry, I don't remember," said Tiffany shortly.

Just then, Katie felt a fairy land on her ponytail. "Don't worry," a voice whispered in her ear. Katie could tell that it was Bluebell. "This is why we worked the fairy magic on her earlier – we had a feeling she might go back on her promise."

Just then, Tiffany shrieked and jumped backwards. She held her hand up in the air and stared at it in horror. Katie gasped when she saw Tiffany's finger. It was the one on which she wore the peridot ring. It had turned bright green and swollen up to the size of a kiwi.

Katie hid her smile. "Give me the ring," she demanded.

"No!" cried Tiffany, and her finger swelled up to the size of an apple. She stared accusingly at Katie. "H-h-how are you doing this?" she cried.

Katie looked her steadily in the eye. "Give me the ring," she repeated.

"No!" yelled Tiffany, and with that her finger swelled up to the size of a melon. Alarmed, Tiffany cried, "All right, you can have it!" and tried to tug the ring off. As soon as she pulled at it, her finger returned to its normal size and colour and the ring slid off. Katie could hear giggling in the air around her and Rosehip whispered in her ear, "Quick, get it before she changes her mind."

Katie held out her hand and Tiffany dropped the ring into her palm, still staring at her finger, wondering if what she'd just seen was real or

not. "How did you—" she began, but Katie and the fairies were gone, hurrying back to Ebony.

Once they were safely round the corner the fairies landed on the stable door and burst into giggles. Bluebell laughed so much she almost fell off! "That was very naughty," said Katie, but she couldn't help smiling too.

Suddenly they heard footsteps coming towards them. The fairies all flew backwards into the stable, thinking it was Tiffany.

But instead it was the girl with the short dark hair. The one who'd clapped so hard when Katie and Ebony had won the Chase Me Charlie. Relieved, Katie gave her a big smile.

"I'm Lily Rose," said the girl shyly. "I've come to see Ebony."

Chapter 6

Lily Rose gave Ebony a huge hug, burying her face in his mane, and he nuzzled into her side contentedly. "Oh, I just love this pony so much," she sighed.

"Me too," said Katie.

Lily Rose straightened up, looking alarmed. "You're not buying him, are you?" she asked.

"Oh no!" cried Katie. "But, is that what *you* want to do?"

Lily Rose hugged Ebony tight

again and nodded. She told Katie that she'd come to the stables with her father, looking for a pony to buy. "I fell in love with Ebony straight away," she explained, "but the owner told us he was bad tempered and dangerous, so Dad wouldn't even let me try riding him."

"He was just lonely and bored," Katie explained. "He'll be fine now. All he wants is someone to love who'll love him back. You're the perfect person."

Lily Rose beamed. "Yes, I am," she said.

Katie caught sight of the hovering fairies. They all had huge grins on their faces.

"I've just got to persuade my dad

that Ebony really is safe," said Lily Rose. "He was impressed with the way he behaved for you, but he wants to see me ride him myself."

In a flash Katie had lent Lily Rose her riding hat and given her a leg-up, and then she and the fairies hurried to the side of the arena to watch, with all their fingers crossed for luck.

Lily Rose rode Ebony brilliantly and when her father said that she could buy him he whinnied with delight – he seemed to understand that he'd found his special friend, without Rosehip even having to translate!

That's when Katie glanced into the car park and saw Tiffany's car driving away. "Oh, stop, wait!" she cried, dashing after it, but the car was soon out of sight. Katie walked back

into the yard, shoulders drooping, trying not to cry. She couldn't believe Tiffany would be so mean as to leave her behind. How on earth was she going to get home now?

Luckily, Lily Rose asked her what was wrong and Katie explained what Tiffany had done. "That's no problem, we'll take you home," said Lily Rose's dad kindly.

So when he'd spoken to the owner about Ebony, and Katie had called Mum from the office to check it was OK to come home with someone else, they set off – but not before the fairies had quickly changed Katie's riding outfit back into her normal clothes. Katie didn't want Mum asking any awkward questions! Too tired out from all the pompom waving to fly, the fairies hitched a lift with Ebony in the horsebox.

When they all arrived at Katie's house, Mum came out to greet them. Katie introduced her to Lily Rose and her dad, and Ebony, of course. "I even had a little ride on him and got this," she told her, holding up her red rosette for Mum to see.

Lily Rose laughed. "Oh, Katie, don't be so modest!" she cried. "It was more than—" She suddenly stopped as Katie gave her a quick shake of her head – she didn't want Mum to know she'd been cantering and jumping in the gymkhana – that would be very difficult to explain!

Before Lily Rose got back in the car, she gave Katie a big hug and invited her to come over any time. "I'd love to see you again," she said, "and so would Ebony."

"Thanks, you too," said Katie merrily.

As they stood waving goodbye, only Katie saw the fairies come whizzing out of the horsebox and zoom high up into the air above them. Mum beamed and pulled her close. "I'm so glad you had fun, darling," she said, "and how wonderful that you've made such a nice new friend! I wish you could go riding every week, but it's just so expensive."

Katie smiled up at Mum and said, "Not to worry, I'm sure I'll get the chance to ride again soon."

She heard giggling at this and glanced around to find the four fairies lounging in the birdbath. She couldn't help grinning too, knowing that she could ride the enchanted ponies in the almost-meadow whenever she liked.

As Mum went indoors to make some tea, Katie hurried over to her friends. She took the peridot ring from her pocket and they all watched it sparkling in the sunshine.

"That's four birthstones we've got," she said proudly. "Maybe we really *can* save the oak tree!"

"Hip hip hooray for Katie!" cried Bluebell, and they all clapped and cheered for her.

"I couldn't have done it without you," she said, "so hooray for the fairies too!"

"Hip hip hooray for the fairies!"

they all cried gleefully, splashing about in the shallow water. Then they all said goodbye and Katie waved and waved to them as they fluttered off high over the roof, back to the almost-meadow and the Fairy House.

And as she wandered indoors, Katie couldn't help wondering what kind of exciting adventure they'd have next.

The End

COME AND JOIN
YOUR FAIRY FRIENDS!

For fantastic competitions,
exclusive material and lots more fairy fun,
enter the Fairy House now!

www.thefairyhouse.co.uk

Bluebell
Spring fairy

Likes:

blue, blue, blue and more blue,
turning somersaults in the air, dancing

Dislikes:

coming second, being told what to do

Daisy
Summer fairy

Likes:

everyone to be friends, bright sunshine,
cheery colours, big fairy hugs

Dislikes:

arguments, cold dark places,
orange nylon dresses

Rosehip
Autumn fairy

Likes:

riding magic ponies, telling Bluebell
what to do, playing the piano, singing

Dislikes:

keeping quiet, boring colours,
not being the centre of attention!

Snowdrop
Winter fairy

Likes:

singing fairy songs, cool quiet places, riding her
favourite magical unicorn, making snowfairies

Dislikes:

being too hot, keeping secrets

Don't miss the rest of the series!

The Fairy House

Fairy Friends

Kelly McKain

Kelly McKain

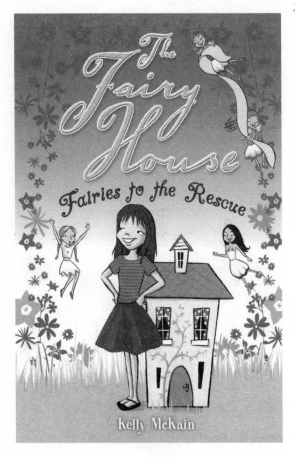